S0-AQC-470

Yucky Science

Chocolate Ants, Maggot Cheese, and More

The Yucky Food Book

Alvin and Virginia Silverstein
and
Laura Silverstein Nunn

Illustrated by
Gerald Kelley

Library of Congress Cataloging-in-Publication Data:

Silverstein, Alvin.

Chocolate ants, maggot cheese, and more : the yucky food book / by Alvin Silverstein, Virginia Silverstein and Laura Silverstein Nunn.

p. cm. — (Yucky science)

Includes bibliographical references and index.

Summary: "Explores 'yucky' foods from around the world, including frog legs, grubs, scrapple, maggot cheese, and more"—Provided by publisher.

ISBN 978-0-7660-3315-3

1. Food habits—Juvenile literature. 2. Food preferences—Juvenile literature. I. Silverstein, Virginia B. II. Nunn, Laura Silverstein. III. Title.

GT2850.S565 2009

394.1'2—dc22

2009012283

Printed in the United States of America

052010 Lake Book Manufacturing, Inc., Melrose Park, IL

10 9 8 7 6 5 4 3 2 1

To Our Readers: We have done our best to make sure all Internet Addresses in this book were active and appropriate when we went to press. However, the author and the publisher have no control over and assume no liability for the material available on those Internet sites or on other Web sites they may link to. Any comments or suggestions can be sent by e-mail to comments@enslow.com or to the address on the back cover.

Enslow Publishers, Inc., is committed to printing our books on recycled paper. The paper in every book contains 10% to 30% post-consumer waste (PCW). The cover board on the outside of each book contains 100% PCW. Our goal is to do our part to help young people and the environment too!

Illustration Credits: © 2009 Gerald Kelley, www.geraldkelley.com

Photo Credits: Associated Press, p. 25; © Joe McDaniel/iStockphoto.com, p. 16; Nature's Images, Inc./Photo Researchers, Inc., p. 14; Peter Menzel/Photo Researchers, Inc., p. 11; Shutterstock, pp. 8, 23, 24, 31, 34, 35, 40, 42.

Cover Illustration: © 2009 Gerald Kelley, www.geraldkelley.com

Enslow Publishers, Inc.
40 Industrial Road
Box 398
Berkeley Heights, NJ 07922
USA
http://www.enslow.com

CONTENTS

What's Yucky?

Worms . . . slime . . . rotting fish . . . Just thinking of these things can make you exclaim, "Eew, gross!" Actually seeing, smelling, or touching yucky things can make you feel like throwing up. And as for eating them . . . would you do it if somebody dared you? *Could* you?

How do you decide something is disgusting? You might get grossed out if a food smells, looks, or feels different from what you're used to. Does that mean it must taste yucky? You probably think certain foods are yucky because they are unfamiliar to you. But while you may want to stay away from these foods, other people may find them delicious and exciting. You might learn to like them, too, after you have tried them a couple of times.

Most Americans these days think foods like fruits, vegetables, grains, nuts, and various meats and dairy products make up a tasty and healthy diet. The meat they eat is mainly muscles from the body and legs of cattle, pigs, fish, and poultry. But they may think organs such as brains and intestines are yucky, and animal parts such as eyes or feet are gross. For most Americans, eating insects, worms, or any kind of animal that is still alive and moving is a real gross-out! Yet, in many countries, foods that are yucky to Americans are an important part of the diet. And people from these countries may think that foods that are familiar to us, such as hot dogs, are yucky!

Are you curious about what "yucky" foods people eat in various parts of the world? Read on for a sampling of disgusting delights. Maybe you'd like to try some of them.

CHAPTER ONE

Crunchy Crawlies

BUGS TO GO

Would you eat a bug if a friend dared you to? In the United States, many people get grossed out just *thinking* about eating a bug. In other countries, however, feasting on crickets or munching on cockroaches is about as natural as eating a cheeseburger or fried chicken in the United States.

What about chocolate covered ants? The chocolate part sounds good, but the *ants*? Chocolate covered ants and other insect candies are often sold in the

Where's the Beef?

A hamburger is loaded with protein, but it may also be loaded with fat. Many insects have a lot more protein than beef, and they have much less fat. A hamburger, for example, may have about 18 percent protein and 18 percent fat. A cooked grasshopper, however, contains as much as 60 percent protein, but only about 6 percent fat.

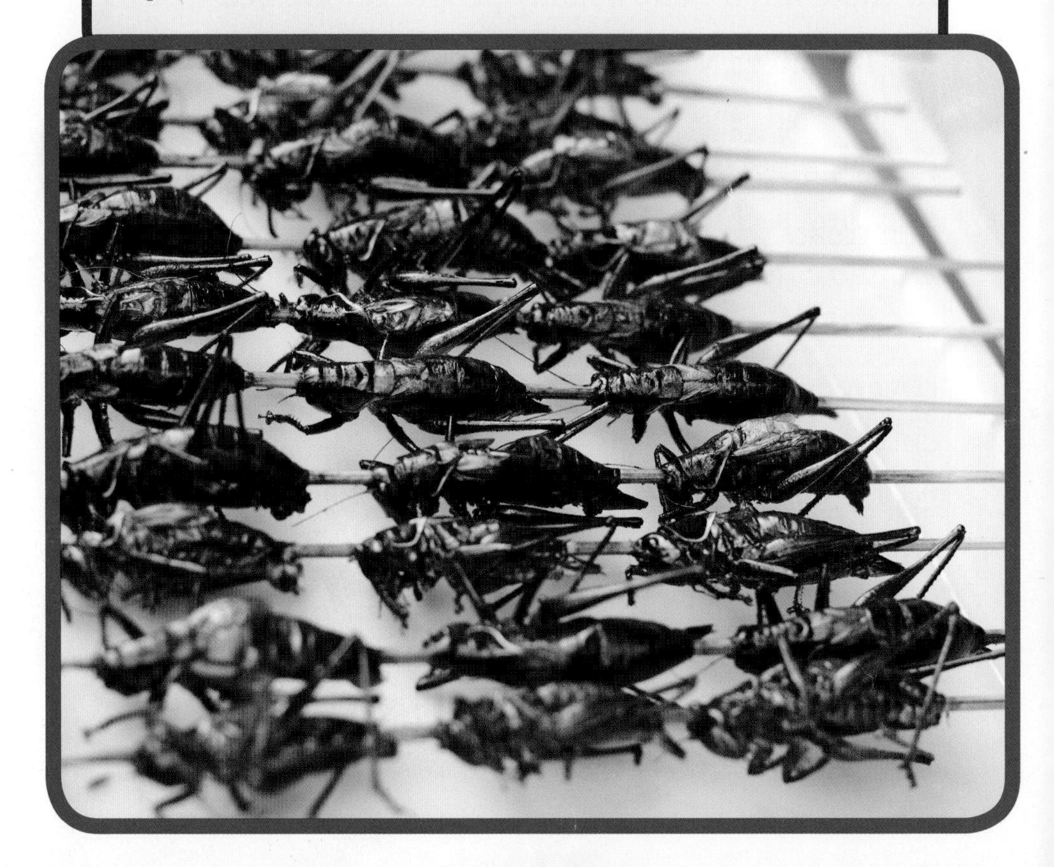

United States as a gag gift, a sort of joke. But in certain parts of the world—such as Central and South America, Africa, Asia, and Australia—eating ants is no joke. In fact, ants, crickets, cockroaches, and other insects are a regular part of the local diet. And why not? Not only are they cheap, but insects are a really good source of protein. Take cockroaches, for example. You may think of them as disgusting creatures that scurry across the kitchen floor at night. But a cockroach snack has three times as much protein as the same amount of chicken.

In some areas, local food markets sell insects by the pound or as deep-fried snacks. In Taiwan, for example, deep-fried crickets are considered a real treat.

Yikes! In the United States, jars of peanut butter may contain extra bits of protein—insect parts that accidentally get processed with the peanuts.

Some restaurants even offer insect entrees. In Thailand, a popular restaurant has sweet vegetable curry with ant eggs on the menu. You can also try crickets in coconut cream and spices wrapped in banana leaves. A restaurant in Singapore offers crispy black ants on shredded potato and vegetables. People in Vietnam use a mixture of fried crickets and peanuts to add flavor to other foods. In Colombia, people in movie theaters might munch on roasted ants instead of popcorn.

CRUNCHY SPIDERS

"Eek! A spider!" If you think eating roasted ants is gross, imagine taking a bite out of a spider. In certain parts of the world, the giant tarantula is a popular snack. This is one of the world's largest spiders, with legs that stretch up to 30 centimeters (nearly 12 inches) long! In Cambodia, food markets along roadsides sell deep-fried tarantulas on a stick.

This young Cambodian woman is eating tarantulas on a stick.

The first step in getting the spiders ready to eat is to remove the fangs. Then the large abdomen is twisted off, and the gooey liquid inside is squeezed out. The rest of the spider is roasted over an open fire for a few minutes. After the spider parts are cooked, people can eat the meat inside the legs, jaws, and head, much as they would eat a crab. The fangs make handy toothpicks!

Yikes! Tarantulas are very hairy spiders. When a tarantula is upset, it will flick off long, needle-like hairs from its abdomen. These hairs are covered with an irritating chemical that can cause a rash. The hairs must be completely burned off before eating. Otherwise, they could irritate the eater's throat.

CHAPTER TWO

Wiggly Snacks

FAT JUICY BITES

Would it bother you to chomp on something that wiggles around in your mouth? In certain parts of the world, some people enjoy munching on wiggly, wormlike creatures.

In Southeast Asia, the sago worm is a favorite treat among native tribes. It has a plump, yellowy-cream body and a hard-shelled head. Despite its name, it's not really a worm, like the earthworm. The sago worm is actually a grub, the young form of the Capricorn beetle. The sago worm got its name because it looks like a short fat worm, and it feeds on the rotting trunks of sago palm plants.

These sago worms are being sauteed with oil and vegetables at a restaurant in Peru.

Some people are adventurous and eat sago worms raw. After washing the worm, they put the wriggling body into their mouths, tail first. Then they bite off the worm's head and throw it away. But others would rather chop off the head with a knife and then pop the grub into their mouths. As they chew, they can feel the creamy insides oozing into their mouth. People who eat sago worms say they are rather tasty. Some say they taste like bacon; others say they taste like shrimp.

Most people would rather eat *cooked* sago worms. They fry the grubs in a hot frying pan. When the "worms" stop wriggling, they're done. They shouldn't be fried too long or the creamy insides will burst out of their fat bodies. Then the best part is gone!

CRUNCHY CATERPILLARS

Have you ever raised a caterpillar in a jar and watched it turn into a butterfly or a moth? These young insects are another favorite food in some parts of the world. The mopane caterpillar, for

Healthy Snack

Grubs make great healthy snacks. They are rich in protein—as much as 70 to 80 percent of their weight!

example, is a very popular food in South African villages. In fact, sales of beef and other meat products drop when the caterpillars are in season during Africa's summer months, from November to January.

The mopane caterpillar is plump and long, growing up to 15 centimeters (6 inches)! Before the villagers cook the caterpillars, they squeeze out the yucky-smelling insides. The caterpillars may be boiled, fried, sun-dried, or smoked. Cooked caterpillars may also be added to a stew.

Many people in Africa eat mopane caterpillars like this one.

Yikes! Not all caterpillars can be eaten. Some are covered with bad-tasting chemicals that can make you very sick. These caterpillars are usually brightly colored, with easy-to-recognize markings. Their bright colors act as warning signs: Don't eat me—or else!

WIGGLY CHEESE

Mother flies lay their eggs in animal poop, rotting garbage, and even the open wounds of living animals. The eggs hatch into young forms called maggots, which look like tiny wiggly worms. After they hatch, the maggots feed on the poop, garbage, or animal flesh. And yet, in some parts of the world, people like to eat maggots!

In Sardinia, Italy, maggot cheese is a special treat, served at weddings and parties. To make it, an open pot of sheep-milk cheese is left out in the sun. A kind of fly known as the "cheese fly" will find it. These flies can smell the cheese from up to 30 meters (100 feet) away, and zoom in to lay their eggs on the cheese. The eggs hatch into wriggly, wormlike maggots. As the maggots grow, they make chemicals that help the cheese rot even faster. If you eat it, watch out! Not only does the cheese stink, taste rotten, and burn the tongue, but the maggots jump. They may hit you right in the eye.

CHAPTER THREE

Leftovers

SPARE PARTS

People who eat meat usually don't mind munching on the legs, ribs, or even rump of a cow. But after the butcher cuts off the steaks and roasts, there's a lot of healthy stuff left over. Many Americans get grossed out at the thought of eating internal organs, such as the brain, heart, liver, kidneys, stomach, and intestines. And yet, some of these leftovers are very nutritious. Take the liver, for example. Liver is chock full of protein, vitamins, and minerals. Liver and onions or paté (chopped liver) might gross you out, but many people think they're yummy delicacies.

Many people around the world don't mind eating an animal's spare parts. For example, you can probably find cow tongue at your local supermarket. It is popular in many countries, including Mexico, Russia, Germany, Japan, and the Philippines. Cow tongue is not healthy like liver, though. It is very high in fat and calories.

Boiled cow tongue (also called beef tongue) can be used in sauces or any food dish that calls for beef. It is often used as meat filling in Mexican food, such as tacos and burritos.

Cow brains are a popular dish for many people who live in France, Spain, Mexico, and Pakistan, as well as certain places in the United States. Cow brains are rather mushy and don't have much flavor. They are usually cooked with seasonings and sauces, such as chili sauce.

In St. Louis, Missouri, a fried brain sandwich was a popular menu item during the late 1800s. The sandwich was made with sliced calves' brains. These days, only a handful of restaurants still offer these sandwiches.

You probably know that ham and bacon come from pigs. But when was the last time you ate pig's feet? That may depend on where you live. In the southern and midwestern United States, pickled pig's feet are very popular. Before pickling, the

Killer Brains

Maybe it's a good thing that eating cow brains is not as popular as it used to be. That's because of mad cow disease, an illness that caused a scare in the mid-1980s to 1990s. The disease attacks the brains of cows. The infected cows eventually die. But some of the sick cows—especially in Great Britain—were killed for food. The disease spread to some people who ate the infected meat. Since then, new rules have been made to prevent the disease from hurting more people.

feet are boiled in water. Then they are stored in big glass jars, filled with hot water mixed with vinegar, salt, and other seasonings. People usually eat the pickled pig's feet as a snack rather than a main meal.

SCRAMBLED PARTS

Do you like sausages? Do you know what's in them? Sausages are usually made from bits of muscle meat and fat that are trimmed off when beef or pork is cut up into steaks, roasts, and chops. But sausages may also contain a mixture of chopped-up animal brains, hearts, livers, lungs, kidneys, stomachs, and tongues. All this stuff is held together by a thin "skin" that may actually be animal intestines!

In Pennsylvania, restaurants serve a popular sausage-like breakfast food known as scrapple. It's their way of keeping pork scraps from going to waste. Scrapple may contain all kinds of pig parts—heart, liver, tongue, brain, and even the head! The pork scraps are ground and then boiled with cornmeal and seasonings until they are mush.

Then they are molded into loaves that can be sliced and fried.

A Scottish dish called haggis is made up of chopped-up sheep parts—lungs, hearts, and livers—mixed together with oatmeal and spices. The mixture then gets stuffed inside the sheep's stomach and boiled for about three hours.

Haggis is a Scottish dish boiled inside a sheep's stomach.

VAMPIRE SPECIAL

We've all heard about vampires—monsters who feed on human blood to survive. Of course, vampires are just a myth. But some people in Africa do drink raw blood. They don't get it from humans, though. The blood usually comes from cows, sheep, and pigs. They mix the animal's blood with milk. It makes a healthy meal!

Does a dish called "blood pudding" sound yucky to you? Also called blood sausage or black pudding, it is made by cooking pig or cow blood with meat, bread, barley, or oatmeal. As it cools, it becomes thick like pudding. In England, Scotland, and Ireland, people eat it for breakfast. What a way to start the day!

Blood pudding is a sausage made with cow's blood.

COFFEE FROM POOP?

Who would pay $50 for a cup of coffee? Some people actually do. Kopi Luwak is a very special kind of coffee made from Indonesian coffee beans. These beans are "pre-treated"—by animals! Palm civets, which look like weasels, eat raw coffee berries. Their digestive system breaks down the bright red outer layer, removing the bitter taste. The inner coffee beans pass out in the civets' poop. Local civet raisers collect the poop and sell the beans to coffee makers. People who have tried Kopi Luwak say it has a very unusual flavor.

Farmers harvest coffee beans for Kopi Luwak from the droppings of civets.

CHAPTER FOUR

The Other White Meat

TASTES LIKE CHICKEN!

People often joke, "It tastes like chicken," when they try an unusual meat for the first time. It isn't always true, but frog legs actually do taste like chicken. They're also a healthy kind of meat, high in protein and low in fat.

The French are famous for eating frog legs. In fact, they eat about twenty thousand frogs per year! Frog legs are also popular in many other countries in Europe, in the southern United States, and in Asia. The kind of frog whose legs are eaten most often is called the "edible frog."

In some Asian countries, edible frogs are raised on frog farms. Most frog legs that people eat in the rest of the world, however, come from wild frogs caught by hunters.

ALLIGATOR ON A STICK

Have you heard scary stories about big alligators in swamps that like to snack on people? Actually, people are more likely to snack on alligators. In southern states such as Florida and Louisiana, alligators are raised on farms. Their tough hides make good leather for shoes, belts, and purses. And their meat makes good eating. Some people say it "tastes like chicken." It's also good for you—high-protein and low-fat.

Alligator meat is often sold at state fairs and festivals. Alligator on a stick—strips of fried alligator meat—is an especially popular treat.

The best-tasting part of an alligator is the tail. The meat in its plump midsection has a much stronger taste. Alligator feet have their fans, too. They're served as "alligator wings."

SNAKE STEAK

Don't mess with a rattlesnake—unless you're having it for dinner. Rattlesnake meat is commonly sold in the southwestern states, especially Texas. You can buy it in cans in other parts of the United States, too. Some people say it "tastes like chicken."

But aren't rattlesnakes and other poisonous snakes dangerous to eat? Not if they're prepared right. The venom (poison) is only in the snake's head. So when the snake's head is cut off, the rest is safe to eat. Like alligator meat, snake meat is especially popular at state fairs and festivals.

Rattlesnake Round-Up

Every year, the state of Texas holds a rattlesnake "round-up." Farmers and ranchers collect huge numbers of Western Diamondback rattlesnakes to help control the rattlesnake population. The event draws thousands of visitors who come to sample the fried rattlesnake and to watch snake handlers entertain the crowds. Since the rattlesnake round-up first opened in 1958, over one hundred tons of rattlesnakes have been captured and eaten.

SNACKING ON SNAILS

Underneath its shell, a snail is a slimy little creature. It leaves a trail of goo wherever it goes. And yet, snails make a famous appetizer in France. They call cooked snails escargot. (Pronounce it "ess-car-GO.")

Snails aren't slimy when you eat them. They're washed thoroughly before cooking and then boiled. The slime drains off with the water.

Escargot (cooked snails) is a popular dish in France.

A snail's big, muscular foot makes up most of its body. That's the part that people cook and eat, after throwing away the head and internal organs. Snail meat itself is very high-protein and low-fat. But escargot and some other popular snail dishes are made with lots of butter, which adds fat to the meal.

Yikes! What's that slimy stuff a snail leaves behind? It's mucus, the same stuff found in the snot from your nose.

CHAPTER FIVE

Sea Food

P.U.! STINKY FISH!

Some people don't like fish because they say it smells too "fishy." So how do you think they'd feel if they got a whiff of a fish that smelled like a garbage dumpster? That's how a lot of people describe a traditional Scandinavian dish called lutefisk. And they say it tastes just as bad as it smells!

Lutefisk is made with cod fish. To prepare the fish, the bones are taken out and the skin is stripped off. After salting the fish, it is hung outside to dry for several weeks until it hardens. Then it is taken inside and soaked in a water and lye mixture for several days. Lye is a strong chemical used in making soap.

To make the fish edible, it must be soaked several more days in plain cold water. Now the lutefisk has a jelly-like covering and may smell like rotten garbage. Finally, it is ready to be boiled or baked. In Norway, lutefisk is served with butter, salt, and pepper. Swedes like to eat it with white sauce and yellow mustard.

Yikes! In Asian countries, restaurants serve many kinds of cooked fish whole on a plate—head, scaly skin, and all. A dish or soup of fish eyes is considered a real treat. Fish eggs are eaten in many parts of the world. In fact, some people will pay a lot of money for caviar—a fancy name for fish eggs! Some of the most expensive caviar sells for more than $3,000 per pound!

Over one hundred years ago, lutefisk was a regular part of the Norwegian and Swedish diet. About the same time, many Scandinavians moved to America. Today, some people joke that these people fled their home country to get away from lutefisk. Lutefisk is no longer as common in Norway and Sweden as it used to be. In fact, it is actually eaten more often in the United

States, especially among Scandinavian Americans living in Wisconsin, Minnesota, and the Pacific Northwest.

EDIBLE EELS

During the summer months in Japan, eel sales in food markets and restaurants jump about 30 percent. That's because many people there know about the Japanese legend that says eating eel meat gives them strength. In the summer, temperatures in Japan can get unbearably hot, and

Grilled eel is a popular dish in Japan.

many people believe that eating eel helps them feel better.

Eels have long, snakelike bodies, but they are not snakes. They are actually fish. People eat them in various ways, such as smoked, stir-fried, or jellied. If they want to enjoy the whole eel experience, restaurants will also serve the meal with a clear soup made from eel livers. The livers are very healthy, but many people don't really like the taste.

WATCH IT SQUIRM!

Would you ever eat anything that was alive? Could you handle it squirming in your mouth and tickling your throat as you swallowed? In Korea, octopus is served alive—sort of. Actually, its slippery arms, or tentacles, are chopped off before

Yikes! Don't bite off more than you can chew! The little suction cups on an octopus's tentacle can attach to the inside of a person's throat on its way down. These little suckers can choke people to death!

serving. They are not exactly alive, but they can keep moving for up to a half hour. They wriggle around like crazy and may even attach their suction cups to the plate!

Once you pop one of the tentacles into your mouth, you can actually feel it wriggling around. You might be able to calm it down by soaking it in soy sauce first.

CHAPTER SIX

Freaky Fruits and Vegetables

STINKY FRUIT

If you let bananas or peaches sit around too long, they will start to stink. That's what happens when fruit gets overripe. But their smell doesn't compare to the stink of durian fruit from Southeast Asia. It is by far the world's smelliest fruit—even when it's not rotten. (It does smell *much* worse when it's overripe, though.) People have compared the durian's smell to rotting meat, old gym socks, or sewage!

Durian is not a very pretty fruit. It is very large—about the size of a football—and it is covered with thick spikes. Despite its stinky reputation, durian fruit is actually very popular

Yikes! In Singapore, it is illegal to bring durian fruit on subways, buses, and taxis because of its horrible smell. The fruit is not allowed in many hotels there, either.

in some parts of Asia. It is also sold in some Asian neighborhoods in the United States. If you can get past the smell, the taste is said to be sweet, syrupy, and delicious—at least to some people. Others say that the taste is as bad as the smell. Love it or hate it, durian fruit is definitely unforgettable.

Durian fruit is spiky and smelly, but some people enjoy the taste!

SEAWEED SALAD

You might think of seaweed as just an annoying, useless weed in the ocean. After all, its long, slimy leaves get tangled around your feet when you go for a swim. And when you throw in a fishing line, the hook comes up full of seaweed. But in some parts of the world, including Asia and Hawaii, "water weeds," such as seaweed and other algae, are used in cooking. Restaurants routinely toss their slippery leaves into salads and soups and cook them with vegetables. In Japan, seaweed is an important ingredient in making a popular

Algae Snot

One type of water weed you *won't* want to toss in your seaweed salad is a kind of algae nicknamed "rock snot." If you haven't guessed by its name, it is really slimy and gooey, and it looks like globs of snot. Rock snot grows on rocks in warm, shallow waters of rivers, streams, and lakes.

In Japanese cuisine, seaweed is often used to wrap sushi.

dish called sushi. Sushi is a Japanese dish of balls of boiled rice rolled in seaweed with raw fish, vegetables, or egg.

Seaweed is very nutritious. It is rich in important vitamins and minerals. It is also low in calories. In fact, celebrities such as Victoria Beckham, supermodel Cindy Crawford, and pop singer Madonna have been known to drink seaweed shakes to help keep in shape.

Which foods in this book made you feel like gagging? Were there any you thought you would like to try? Remember, what might seem yucky to you may be considered delicious by somebody else.

Will ants, spiders, grubs, or snails ever be popular foods in the United States? Actually, many people are probably eating these things in the United States already—maybe even in your neighborhood!

Some scientists say that eating bugs would be a great way to live. Bugs are very nutritious and low in fat. They are also very affordable and easy to farm, compared to cows and chickens. Could bugs on our dinner plates be in our future?

WORDS TO KNOW

edible Describing anything that can be used as food.

grub The wormlike form that hatches from the egg of beetles and other insects. It later changes into the adult form.

haggis A Scottish dish made of sheep's internal organs mixed with oatmeal and spices and boiled in the animal's stomach.

lutefisk A Scandinavian dish made of codfish soaked in a lye mixture.

lye A harsh chemical often used to make soap.

mad cow disease A fatal illness spread by eating the brains of infected cattle.

maggot The young form of the housefly.

mucus A slimy fluid that coats and protects the inside of the mouth, nose, throat, and other parts of the body; or, slimy covering on a living creature, such as a snail or a worm, to keep the animal from drying out.

protein One of the substances that is found in all living cells of animals and plants. It is necessary for growth and life.

scrapple Pork scraps cooked with cornmeal and seasonings, formed into a loaf and cooled. It is sliced before serving.

sushi A Japanese dish made of a ball of cooked rice rolled in seaweed with raw fish, vegetables, or egg.

venom Poison, especially of a spider or a snake.

FURTHER READING

Rosenberg, Pam. *Eek! Icky, Sticky, Gross Stuff in Your Food*. Mankato, Minn.: Child's World, 2007.

Schlaht, Kim. *Ronnie's Rotten Recipes.* Moreno Valley, Calif.: TICO Publishing, 2006.

Swanson, Diane. *Burp! The Most Interesting Book You'll Ever Read About Eating*. Toronto: Kids Can Press, 2001.

INTERNET ADDRESSES

DLTK. "Burns Night (Scotland)."

<http://www.dltk-kids.com/world/scotland/burnsnight.htm/>

Weird-food.com. "Weird Food & Strange Food from Around the World."

<http://www.weird-food.com/>

Index